First published in 2007 by
Franklin Watts
338 Euston Road
London
NW1 3BH

Franklin Watts Australia
Level 17/207 Kent Street
Sydney
NSW 2000

A CIP catalogue record for this book is available
from the British Library.

ISBN 978 0 7496 7155 6 (hbk)
ISBN 978 0 7496 7298 0 (pbk)

Series Editor: Jackie Hamley
Series Advisor: Dr Hilary Minns
Series Designer: Peter Scoulding

Printed in China

Franklin Watts is a division of
Hachette Children's Books.

Sam's Sunflower

by Jillian Powell

Illustrated by Johanna Boccardo

FRANKLIN WATTS
LONDON • SYDNEY

Jillian Powell

"I once grew sunflowers in pots on a roof garden. They are lovely big seeds to grow. Mine grew so tall the wind kept blowing them over!"

Johanna Boccardo

"I love flowers, and so does my beautiful cat, Matilda. When I try to plant any flowers at home, Matilda eats them. Sunflowers are our favourite!"

Class 2B were
growing sunflowers.

There was a prize
for the tallest.

First they sowed
the seeds.

Then they watered them.

Soon the sunflowers were growing ...

Jack

am

Pat

... except for Sam's.

They all grew taller ...

... except for Sam's.

"Perhaps a bird took the seed," the teacher said to Sam.

But there was something growing behind the wall.

It was Sam's
sunflower!

Everyone came and
looked up at it.

Sam's sunflower
was the tallest
of all!

Notes for adults

TADPOLES are structured to provide support for newly independent readers. The stories may also be used by adults for sharing with young children.

Starting to read alone can be daunting. **TADPOLES** help by providing visual support and repeating words and phrases. These books will both develop confidence and encourage reading and rereading for pleasure.

If you are reading this book with a child, here are a few suggestions:

1. Make reading fun! Choose a time to read when you and the child are relaxed and have time to share the story.

2. Talk about the story before you start reading. Look at the cover and the blurb. What might the story be about? Why might the child like it?

3. Encourage the child to reread the story, and to retell the story in their own words, using the illustrations to remind them what has happened.

4. Discuss the story and see if the child can relate it to their own experience, or perhaps compare it to another story they know.

5. Give praise! Remember that small mistakes need not always be corrected.

**If you enjoyed this book,
why not try another TADPOLES story?**

Sammy's Secret
978 0 7496 6890 7

Mop Top
978 0 7946 6895 2

Stroppy Poppy
978 0 7496 6893 8

Charlie and the Castle
978 0 7496 6896 9

I'm Taller Than You!
978 0 7496 6894 5

Over the Moon!
978 0 7496 6897 6

Leo's New Pet
978 0 7496 6891 4

My Sister is a Witch!
978 0 7496 6898 3